How to Trick the Tooth Fairy

How to Trick the Tooth Fairy

By Erin Danielle Russell

Illustrated by Jennifer Hansen Rolli

SIMON & SCHUSTER

London   New York   Sydney   Toronto   New Delhi

SIMON & SCHUSTER
First published in Great Britain in 2018 by Simon & Schuster UK Ltd ‣ 1st Floor, 222 Gray's Inn Road, London, WC1X 8HB ‣ A CBS Company ‣ Originally published in 2018 by Aladdin, an imprint of Simon & Schuster Children's Publishing Division, New York ‣ Text copyright © 2018 Erin Danielle Russell ‣ Illustrations copyright © 2018 Jennifer Hansen Rolli ‣ The right of Erin Danielle Russell and Jennifer Hansen Rolli to be identified as the author and illustrator of this work has been asserted by them in accordance with the Copyright, Designs and Patents Act, 1988 ‣ All rights reserved, including the right of reproduction in whole or in part in any form ‣ A CIP catalogue record for this book is available from the British Library upon request ‣ 978-1-4711-6026-4 (PB) ‣ 978-1-4711-6027-1 (EB) ‣ Printed in China ‣ 1 2 3 4 5 6 7 8 9 10

To my mom and dad for all their love, help, and encouragement.
Thank you for believing in me!

And to the Tooth Fairy for all the magical years
of dollar bills and fairy-dust cookies

—E. D. R.

★ ☆ ★

To my dear sisters, Heather and Beth,
who were all too often the deliverers of tricky treats

—J. H. R.

Kaylee *loved* to pull pranks.

Prank princess in training

Twinkle of mischief

Favourite holiday is April Fool's Day

Cute as a button, sharp as a tack

Comfy shoes for creeping

She pulled pranks every day . . .

every night . . .

and even on holidays.

She was *always* looking for her
next unsuspecting victim.

But was Kaylee
the princess
of pranks?

No.

That would be this little trickster . . .

THE TOOTH FAIRY!

Ruling prank
princess

Smirky
smile

Fairy wings for
a quick getaway

More tricks
in her bag than teeth

Magical tooth
grabber

But she had no clue who she was about to meet....

Shhhhhhhhhh

The Tooth Fairy was
expecting to find something
small, smooth and white,

not green with webbed feet!

EEEEEEK!

Now, if you prank the Tooth Fairy
with a *fake* frog, you'll get . . .

REAL FROGS!

Had Kaylee finally met
her mischief-making match?

She offered the Tooth Fairy a slice of pie.

And if you know anything about fairies, you know they LOOOOOVE sweets.

The Tooth Fairy
dug into her dessert.
Suddenly her mouth
was on fire!

Now, if you prank
the Tooth Fairy
with prankster pie,
she'll top it with . . .

GOBS OF GOOEY
ICE CREAM!

Kaylee was a mess!

Pass the sprayer, please.

But once the sprayer was in her hands, Kaylee turned it on the Tooth Fairy!

Whoooooooooooooshhhhhhh

Now, if you prank the Tooth Fairy with a splash of water, she'll make it . . .

rain . . .

Storms scared Kaylee!
She ran and hid behind a closet door.

The Tooth Fairy wanted to out-prank Kaylee,
but frightening her wasn't fun at all.

Kaylee sprang out of hiding, surprising the Tooth Fairy with a burst of bubble gum.

And if you know
anything about tooth
fairies, you know
a broken
wand means . . .

TOPSY-TURVY

TOOTH FAIRY TROUBLE!

Kaylee and the Tooth Fairy may have been
soaked
and scared
and stunned.

But
luckily . . .

Kaylee had one more trick
up her pyjama sleeve.

And so did the
Tooth Fairy...

Bye-bye,
little furballs!

And together,
they cleaned up
their mess.

Now, if you know
anything about pranksters
and fairies . . .

you know there's room for lots
of fairy-dust cookies,

two prank
princesses,

and one new
friendship.

I think my
tooth is loose.